Katie Meets the Impressionists

JAMES MAYHEW

SCHOLASTIC INC.

New York   Toronto   London   Auckland   Sydney
Mexico City   New Delhi   Hong Kong   Buenos Aires

For my sister, the original "Katie"
—J.M.

To find out more about Impressionist painters, turn to the end of the book.

This book was originally published in Great Britain in 1997 by Orchard Books London, and in the United States in 1999 by Orchard Books.

ISBN-13: 978-0-439-93508-1
ISBN-10: 0-439-93508-3

12 11 10 9 8 7 6 5 4 3   8 9 10 11 12/0

Printed in the U.S.A.   08

First Bookshelf edition, May 2007

Book design by Mina Greenstein
The text of this book is set in 14 point Galliard. The illustrations are watercolor.

It was Grandma's birthday, and for a special treat she took
Katie to the art museum.

Katie loved the museum, because you never knew what you
were going to see there.

"Look at the flowers in the paintings," said Grandma.

"I can only see spots," said Katie.

"The pictures are made up of dabs of paint and color," said
Grandma. "But when you stand back, the dabs make a picture."

Katie wandered off into the next room to try. There she saw a painting called *The Luncheon* by Claude Monet. When she stood back, Katie could see a garden.

Grandma would love flowers like those for her birthday, she thought. She closed her eyes and sniffed. She was sure she could smell the flowers.

And when Katie opened her eyes, there she was, among the daisies, hollyhocks, roses, and sunflowers.

"Can I pick some flowers?" said Katie to the little boy, whose name was Jean.

Jean called his mother and nanny over, and spoke to them in French.

"*Un bouquet?*" said his mother. "*Oui,* Jean, you go and help the girl."

So Jean and Katie gathered flowers together.

"Are you going to paint them?" he asked.

"No, they are for my grandma," said Katie.

"Papa paints flowers," said Jean. "I'll show you."

Jean took Katie to a room full of pictures, like a small gallery. "This is Papa's studio," he said. "He's a famous painter. His name is Claude Monet."

"I'm good at painting," said Katie. "Let's try it."

Using brushes, they mixed the paint on palettes and found canvases to paint on.

They painted portraits of each other, using dabs just like real painters.

"Now I'd better get back to Grandma," said Katie, and they went out into the garden.

"Will you come another day?" asked Jean.

"I'd like to," said Katie. She picked up the bunch of flowers and, waving good-bye, climbed through the frame into the museum.

Katie saw that the bunch of flowers was beginning to wilt. "What I need is some water," she said, looking around the gallery.

She saw a painting called *Girl with a Watering Can* by Pierre Auguste Renoir. Katie looked around to make sure no one was watching her, and climbed inside.

"Can I have some water for my flowers?" said Katie.
The little girl put the flowers into her watering can.
"Voilà!" she said. But the flowers still drooped and
flopped over.

"Come and pick some more!" said the girl.

So Katie and the girl trampled through the garden picking flowers. Katie pretended it was a jungle and that she was a panther chasing the girl.

Suddenly there was a terrible scream. It was the girl's mother. "You have ruined my garden!" she shouted.

"It wasn't me," said the girl. "It was her," and she pointed at Katie.

"Come here, you naughty child," said the mother.

But Katie ran for the picture frame and leapt into the museum, leaving the flowers scattered behind her.

Katie sighed. She didn't dare go back to fetch the
flowers. She went to look at the other pictures. There
were a lot of pictures by Monet.

Katie looked at one called *Field of Poppies*. Wasn't
that Jean, the painter's son, walking through the field?
Katie climbed in to see.

It *was* Jean! He was delighted to see her.

"We're going on a picnic!" he said, and Jean's mother said that Katie could join them.

They walked together, through the poppy field, looking for somewhere to sit.

Jean helped Katie gather armfuls of poppies for Grandma.

Afterward they sat in the shade of the tree, the perfect place for a picnic. Mrs. Monet opened a bag. She had bread and cheese and strawberries.

But Jean heard a buzzing noise and looked up. A black cloud of bees was flying toward them.

"They're after my poppies!" shouted Katie, her mouth full of strawberries.

Jean and his mother ran toward the poppy field. But Katie ran to the picture frame and dived into the museum.

The bees followed Katie, who ran on and on until she reached a
window. She flung it open and threw the poppies out. The bees
flew after them. Katie panted until she got her breath back. She still
didn't have any flowers for Grandma!

She saw another picture by Pierre Auguste Renoir. It showed a girl at the theater and was called *Her First Evening Out*. This girl was holding a posy of flowers.

"Grandma would love a posy like that," said Katie, before jumping into the picture.

"May I have your flowers?" asked Katie. "I'll swap my hair ribbon."

"Hush," said the girl. "The ballet is about to begin!"

Katie looked for a seat, but they were all full. The theater manager appeared.

"*Mademoiselle,* may I see your ticket?" he said.

Katie didn't have one, so she ran off, down some steps.

She could hear the manager coming after her, so she opened a door to hide and stumbled upon some people in bright costumes. When they started shouting at her, she ran the other way, toward some bright lights and the sound of music.

Katie pushed past heavy velvet curtains—and
found herself on stage! The dancers held their
breath. So did the musicians in the orchestra. So did
the audience. What was Katie going to do?

Katie danced! The music started up again, and Katie pranced all
around the stage.

How the audience loved her! They had never seen anyone dance like
that before. They cheered and clapped and threw flowers. Hundreds of
flowers fell upon Katie as she twirled around.

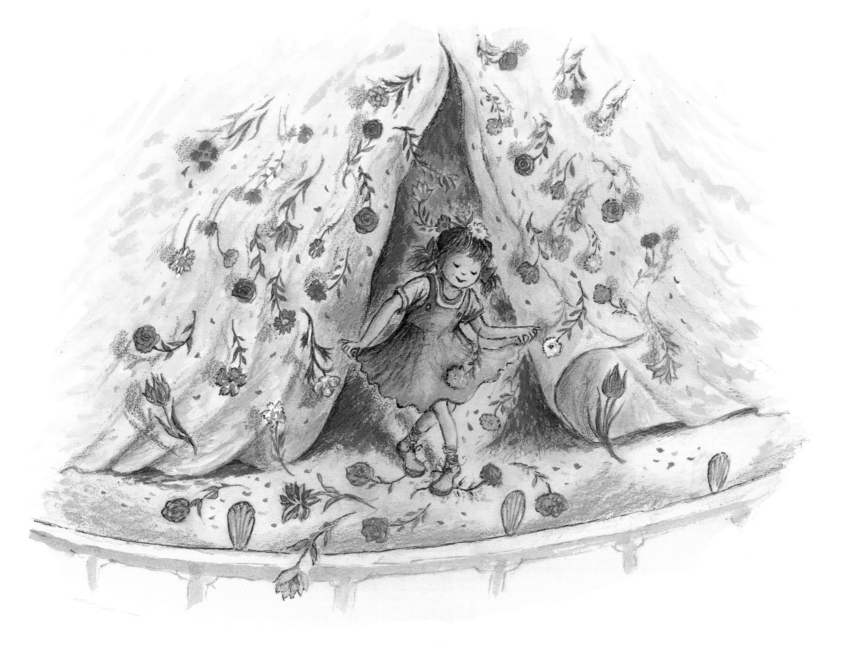

"Well done!" they shouted. "Bravo!"
When the music stopped, Katie curtsied and gathered
up her flowers.

The manager rushed over to her. "My dear, you have such talent!"

Katie blushed. "I just jumped around a bit, really," she said.

"You must dance every night; you will be famous!" said the manager.

"Thanks, but it's Grandma's birthday," said Katie. "I must get back."

But Katie could not find her way to the picture frame. There were people everywhere, changing costumes. She was afraid she might be stuck in the theater picture forever!

All of a sudden she saw another frame.

"I must be in another picture!" said Katie. She gathered up her bouquet and climbed into the museum.

Katie looked back at the picture. *The Blue Dancers* by Edgar Degas, she read. "I wonder if I would have been painted if I had stayed still long enough!" she said.

Then Katie ran over to her grandma and gave her the flowers. "Happy birthday, Grandma!"

"My goodness!" said Grandma. "Wherever did you get these lovely flowers?"

Katie just laughed. But what was that in her pocket? A paintbrush! Monet will need that, she thought.

She ran back to the first picture, left the brush on the frame, and then ran to catch up with her grandma.

MORE ABOUT THE IMPRESSIONISTS

The Impressionist painters lived in France at the end of the nineteenth century and the beginning of the twentieth century. Their paintings tried to capture a particular moment in time (rather like a photograph) by recording an instant "impression." They painted their families, their gardens, trips to the theater, and all sorts of things they saw around them. Often they painted outside in the open air.

Their paintings, made up of dabs of color, were thought to be very modern and ugly at first. Eventually people grew to love their "impressions" because they were full of color and movement, just like things in real life.

CLAUDE MONET (1840–1926)

Monet loved to paint gardens, landscapes, and his family. He painted *The Luncheon* and *Field of Poppies,* which are both in the Musée d'Orsay in Paris, France.

PIERRE AUGUSTE RENOIR (1841–1919)

Renoir was famous for painting portraits, especially of women and children. *Girl with a Watering Can* is in the National Gallery of Art in Washington, D.C., and *Her First Evening Out* is in the National Gallery in London, England.

EDGAR DEGAS (1834–1917)

Degas often painted ballerinas, orchestras, and theaters. He even made statues of ballet dancers. *The Blue Dancers* is in the Musée d'Orsay in Paris, France.

Paintings by these and other great Impressionist artists can be found in museums and galleries all over the world.

ACKNOWLEDGMENTS

The Luncheon by Claude Monet, Musée d'Orsay; © Photo RMN—H. Lewandowski (p. 5)

Girl with a Watering Can by Pierre Auguste Renoir, Chester Dale Collection; © Board of Trustees, National Gallery of Art, Washington, D.C. (p. 10)

Field of Poppies by Claude Monet, Musée d'Orsay; © Photo RMN—H. Lewandowski (p. 15)

Her First Evening Out by Pierre Auguste Renoir, reproduced by courtesy of the Trustees of the National Gallery, London (p. 21)

The Blue Dancers by Edgar Degas, Musée d'Orsay; © Photo RMN—Préveral (p. 30)